When Padayappa Walked the Path of Lord Rama

When Padayappa Walked the Path of Lord Rama

TURNING LOSS, EXILE, AND DEFEAT INTO VICTORY AND PROSPERITY

RAM SWARAJYA

PAPER TOWNS
PUBLISHERS

PAPER TOWNS
PUBLISHERS

First published by

Papertowns Publishers
72, Vishwanath Dham Colony,
Niwaru Road, Jhotwara,
Jaipur, 302012

When Padayappa Walked the Path of Lord Rama

ISBN Print Book – 978-93-6185-021-9

Cover Design by Vidhisha Sharma

@nivarts_ instagram

Email- vidhishasharma95@gmail.com

Printed in India

DEDICATION

This book is dedicated to all those who faced loss but did not lose **Values**.

To those who were pushed aside but did not give up **dignity**.

To those who chose **patience** over anger, and **character** over shortcuts.

May this story remind every reader that *true victory begins within.*

CONTENTS

ABOUT THE BOOK

This mini-book, "*When Padayappa Walked the Path of Lord Rama,*" connects the journey of Padayappa, a powerful film character, with the life and values of Lord Rama from the Ramayana.

Both face loss, injustice, exile, and humiliation. Both choose patience, self-respect, and duty instead of anger or revenge.

Written in simple English, the book shows how a strong character can overcome difficult situations.

It explains how silence can be strength, how waiting can be wisdom, and how right actions bring lasting success.

This is not just a story about the past or a movie character.

It is a guide for anyone facing setbacks in life.

ABOUT THE AUTHOR

Ram SwaRajya is a writer who believes that character is the foundation of success.

Power, position, and fame may change, but values remain constant.

Inspired by Indian epics, cinema, and real-life experiences, the writing blends ancient wisdom with modern life.

Through this book, the author shares a clear message. Loss can become preparation. Silence can be strength.

When one walks the path of Dharma with patience and courage, life slowly turns defeat into victory.

Chapter 1

Chatting About the Book

During their college vacation, Nidhi and Harshada were chatting online.

They were talking about a new book Nidhi had just discovered.

Nidhi: Hey, Harshada! I found a cool book. The title is *"When Padayappa Walked the Path of Lord Rama."* 😳

Harshada: Padayappa walking like Lord Rama? 😂 Did he go into the forest first?

Nidhi: Haha! Maybe! But the subtitle is interesting too: *"Turning Loss, Exile, and Defeat into Victory and Prosperity."*

Harshada: Wow… that sounds serious. Is it a movie story or life lessons?

Nidhi: Both! Padayappa faces betrayal, loss, and humiliation… just like Lord Rama in the Ramayana.

Harshada: Wait… the guy who slaps people with style is now a model of patience and Dharma? 😆

Nidhi: Yes! It's about staying calm, patient, and strong inside. Even when life goes wrong, good character wins.

Harshada: So… basically, don't lose your cool, don't take shortcuts, and Karma helps you?

Nidhi: Exactly! And it's written in simple English. No complicated words.

Harshada: I like it! Finally, I can learn life lessons while feeling like I'm watching a movie! 😄

Chapter 2

Movie Plans

Nidhi and Harshada continued chatting online.

Nidhi: Harshada! Guess what! The classic Indian Tamil-language film *Padayappa* from 1999 is releasing in theatres again! 🎬

Harshada: What? After more than 25 years? 😂 Are the theatres serving time-travel popcorn too?

Nidhi: Haha! No, silly! It's a special release on 12th December 2025 for the Indian superstar Rajinikanth's birthday.

Harshada: Wow… that's awesome! But why do we need to watch it? We can just read the book.

Nidhi: Actually, I was thinking… let's watch the movie first. Then we read the book. It will be easier to understand the story.

Harshada: Hmm… good idea. I want to see Padayappa in action. And maybe learn some life lessons while enjoying the slaps! 😆

Nidhi: Exactly! Plus, it will be fun to see how the movie shows patience, dignity, and courage, just like Lord Rama.

Harshada: Wow… so a movie with style, action, and philosophy? Sign me up! 😄

Nidhi: Let's plan then. Tomorrow evening, theatre nearby. Popcorn ready. Lessons of life incoming!

Harshada: Haha! I hope I don't get inspired so much that I start meditating in class tomorrow. 🧘

Nidhi: Don't worry… we'll start small. First, watch. Then read. Then… maybe meditate after exams! 😄

And just like that, the two friends made their plan. They would watch *Padayappa* on the big screen first, laugh, cheer, and then connect it with the book to see how life lessons come alive in both stories.

Chapter 3

Watching Padayappa

The next evening, Nidhi and Harshada reached the theatre. The hall was full of fans. Posters of Rajinikanth smiled from every wall.

Harshada: Wow! Look at this crowd! I feel like we are in a festival, not a movie hall. 🎉

Nidhi: Haha! Rajinikanth fans are always like this. Get ready for some style, drama, and big action. 😆

The lights dimmed, and the movie started. Padayappa entered the screen with his usual charm and confidence.

Harshada: Whoa! He walks like he owns the Earth! 😮

Nidhi: See? That's exactly why the book compares him to Lord Rama. Even in trouble, he stays calm and strong.

As the story unfolded, betrayal, loss, and challenges came one after another. Padayappa never lost his dignity.

Harshada: Haha! And he slaps the villains in style! But… it's also inspiring. He never cheats or takes shortcuts.

Nidhi: Exactly! Just like Lord Rama. Even when everything goes wrong, the right actions win in the end.

They laughed, cheered, and sometimes clapped loudly at the big scenes. But inside, both were thinking about the lessons hidden in the drama.

Harshada: Nidhi… I never thought a movie could teach so much about patience and courage. 😳

Nidhi: That's why we are watching it before reading the book. Now, when we read, every scene will make sense.

Harshada: Hmm… I think I want to be like Padayappa too. Calm, strong, and… stylish! 😎

Nidhi: Haha! Step one: watch the movie. Step two: learn life lessons. Step three: try the style at home—carefully.

The movie ended, but the excitement stayed. Nidhi and Harshada left the theatre inspired, laughing, and ready to dive into the book, eager to discover more about Padayappa and the path of Lord Rama.

Chapter 4

The Cafe Research

After watching the movie, Nidhi and Harshada walked to a nearby cafe. They ordered coffee and sat at a corner table.

Nidhi: Okay, now the real research begins! 😎 Let's check what the internet says about *Padayappa*.

Harshada: Haha! College won't give us marks for this, but life… maybe! 📱

They opened Wikipedia and started scrolling.

Nidhi: Wow… Padayappa was released on 10th April 1999. It starred Rajinikanth, Ramya Krishnan, and Soundarya. Music by A. R. Rahman.

Harshada: I didn't know Rahman Sir composed the music. No wonder the songs are amazing! 🎶

Nidhi: Look at this! Padayappa was the first Tamil movie released worldwide with 210 prints and 700,000 audio cassettes. That's huge for 1999!

Harshada: Whoa… global superstar vibes! 🌍 Rajinikanth really went worldwide before Instagram existed.

Nidhi: And Ramya Krishnan's Neelambari, the villain was scary but amazing. Won awards too.

Harshada: Yeah… her revenge scenes were intense!

Nidhi: Oh, and check this. Remember the swing scene? Neelambari didn't leave any chairs for Padayappa to sit. So he **pulled the oonjal (swing) with his shawl and sat calmly**.

Harshada: Haha! That was so stylish! But is there a deeper meaning?

Nidhi: Yes! In a 2016 interview with *The Hindu*, director K. S. Ravikumar said this scene was inspired by a sequence in the Ramayana. Hanuman makes a seat for himself using his tail after Ravana does not provide him a chair to sit in Lanka. It's about dignity, cleverness, and calmness when disrespected.

Harshada: Wow… so even a swing scene teaches patience and clever thinking! 😮

Nidhi: Exactly! And the movie also shows courage, forgiveness, and doing the right thing—even for enemies.

Harshada: Hmm… so all the style, slaps, and drama also have life lessons. Who knew scrolling Wikipedia could be so inspiring? 😄

Nidhi: Haha! This is like a research project for life. No college marks, but maybe big marks from destiny!

Harshada: True! Let's finish our coffee and then read the book. I feel like every Wikipedia fact makes the story even cooler.

The two friends smiled. Watching the movie and reading the facts made them ready to dive into the book.

Life lessons were hiding everywhere—on the screen, in the music, and even in a Wikipedia page.

Sources:

- Wikipedia – "Padayappa" (https://en.wikipedia.org/wiki/Padayappa)
- *The Hindu*, 2016 interview with K. S. Ravikumar

Chapter 5

The First Lesson

The next morning, Nidhi and Harshada met at Nidhi's home.

They sat on the sofa, books and notebooks spread around, ready to read.

Nidhi: Okay, first chapter. Let's see what the book says.

Harshada: Hmm… I feel like I am about to start a school assignment… except no marks. Only life points! 😄

They opened the book "*When Padayuppa Walked the Path of Lord Ramu*" and began reading.

Nidhi: The first lesson is about **loss and patience**. Both Padayappa and Lord Rama lose things they love. Padayappa loses family property and faces humiliation. Lord Rama loses his kingdom and is sent to the forest.

Harshada: True… I remember in the movie, Padayappa never shouted or fought unfairly. He stayed calm and planned carefully.

Nidhi: Exactly! The book says: *"Anger and revenge can never give lasting victory. Patience, courage, and dignity do."*

Harshada: Hmm… so even when life seems unfair, it's better to stay strong inside rather than take shortcuts or get angry.

Nidhi: Yes! And look, it also talks about **character over position**. Padayappa could have used his family wealth to fight, but he chooses honesty and cleverness. Lord Rama could have used power to punish, but he follows Dharma.

Harshada: Wow… so calm, smart, and fair wins in the end. I think this is why the movie felt inspiring, not just entertaining.

Nidhi: Exactly. And this book explains it in simple language. Anyone can read and understand it. No complicated philosophy, just real-life lessons.

Harshada: Hmm… I like this. I feel like I am learning without feeling like studying. And maybe I can apply this… in college, with friends… and life in general.

Nidhi: Yep! That's the point. Life will test you, sometimes unfairly. But how you respond matters more than what happens.

Harshada: Wow… so first lesson: **loss happens, stay patient, stay strong, and your character will win.** Got it!

They smiled at each other, feeling a little wiser. The movie, the Wikipedia research, and now the book—all were teaching the same thing: **life is about dignity, patience, and courage, no matter what challenges come.**

Chapter 6

Betrayal and Bad Guys

The next afternoon, Nidhi and Harshada met at a small cafe.

The smell of fresh filter coffee filled the air, and they both grabbed their cups.

Harshada: Okay, chapter two. What's next? I hope it's not another long lecture about patience… I already feel sleepy. 😴

Nidhi: Haha! Don't worry. This one is about **betrayal and injustice**. You know, when people cheat you, lie, or try to mess things up for you.

Harshada: Ohhh… like Suryaprakash and Neelambari trying to ruin Padayappa's life? Total villains. 😆

Nidhi: Exactly! The book says: *"When people betray you, it's tempting to fight back with anger or tricks. But Padayappa shows us how to act smart, not mean."*

Harshada: Hmm… so basically, don't go full villain mode even when someone is mean? 😬

Nidhi: Yes! You can defend yourself, but don't ruin your own character. Padayappa forgave people when they admitted mistakes and even helped them when needed.

Harshada: Hmm… forgive, but don't forget. Got it. And plan smart, like Padayappa. Maybe even with a bit of swag. 😎

Nidhi: Exactly! And Lord Rama handled betrayal the same way. Kaikeyi sent him to the forest unfairly. He didn't fight or cheat her. He stayed calm and did the right thing.

Harshada: Wow… so even epic heroes deal with mean people and still stay cool. I like that.

Nidhi: And it's fun too! You can laugh at the movie scenes, but secretly learn how to handle tricky situations in real life.

Harshada: Haha! So next time someone cheats in a game or spreads a rumor, I'll stay calm, plan, and maybe give them a stylish "oops, I win" move. 😏

Nidhi: Perfect! That's the lesson. Outsmart, don't get angry, and always keep your style and dignity.

They both laughed and sipped their coffee. The book was already teaching life lessons, but in a way they could understand, remember, and maybe even use in college drama, friendships, and everyday life.

Chapter 7

Rising Again and Living in Style

It was a sunny December afternoon. Nidhi and Harshada sat under a big tree in the college courtyard, each sipping fresh coconut water from a vendor nearby.

Harshada: Ah… nothing like fresh coconut water! Better than those bottled juices. Healthy, refreshing… and Rajini style. 😎

Nidhi: Haha! Totally. Rajinikanth would approve. *"Kashtapadama Edhuvum Kidaikkathu. Kashtapadama Kidaikirathu Ennikkum Nilakkathu"*—you know, the punch dialogue from *Padayappa*: "You cannot gain anything without hard work, and what is gained without effort will not last."

Harshada: Haha! So basically, no shortcuts in life. Even if someone wants to become popular overnight… nope, work hard, like Padayappa.

Nidhi: Exactly! And look at how he started over. He lost property, faced humiliation, but stayed calm, worked smart, and rebuilt everything — business, respect, and family.

Harshada: Hmm… so even if exams fail, friendships break, or people gossip, we can rise again. Be calm, work hard, and earn respect.

Nidhi: Yep! And remember the dialogue, *"En Vazhi Thani Vazhi"*—"My way is a unique way." It's like saying: Don't just copy others. Find your own path, even if it's tough.

Harshada: Haha! So don't just follow trends on Facebook or Instagram. Make your own style, your own way, like Padayappa. 😎

Nidhi: And healthy habits, like drinking coconut water instead of sugary drinks… simple things matter too. It's part of staying strong for the long journey.

Harshada: True! I like it. Even a tiny action can be a step toward your own "kingdom," like Padayappa. Work, patience, good health, and loyal friends.

Nidhi: And loyal friends matter. Padayappa had long-term friends who supported him. Rama had Hanuman and his allies in Ayodhya. Life is easier with people who care.

Harshada: Hmm… so punch dialogues in movies are not just style—they're real-life advice. Work hard, find your own way, stay healthy, and value good friends.

Nidhi: Exactly! That's why the book connects Padayappa and Lord Rama. Both faced losses, stayed smart, and built something lasting—family, respect, and prosperity.

They laughed, finishing their coconuts. The sun shone brightly, and the air felt full of energy. They felt inspired, ready to face life with **strength, style, and their own unique path**.

Chapter 8

Staying Calm, Controlling Anger, and Walking the Right Path

It was another sunny afternoon. Nidhi and Harshada sat on a bench near the college gate, sipping fresh coconut water.

Harshada: Ah… coconut water again. Better than bottled soda or juice. Keeps you cool and healthy. Rajini style, you know. 😎

Nidhi: Haha! Totally. And today's lesson from the book is about **controlling anger and handling difficult people**.

Harshada: Oh… like Neelambari in the movie? That beautiful and stylish woman was furious all the time! 😅

Nidhi: Exactly! The book explains how Padayappa **never lost his calm**, even when people insulted him, betrayed him, or tried to harm his family. He always acted wisely and with dignity.

Harshada: Hmm… so basically, don't fight with everyone who is rude. Think smart.

Nidhi: Yes! Remember the punch dialogue, *"Anger is the cause of all miseries. One should know how to control it, otherwise life will become miserable"*? That's directly from the movie, and it's like Lord Rama's teaching too.

Harshada: True! Think about the time when Ravana kidnapped Sita. Rama didn't just lose control or act in anger blindly. He planned carefully, built alliances, and fought wisely to rescue her.

Nidhi: Exactly! And Padayappa did the same! When his uncle tried to cheat him, or Neelambari plotted revenge, Padayappa didn't attack blindly. He acted with patience, cleverness, and fairness—just like Lord Rama.

Harshada: Wow… so Padayappa literally walked the path of Lord Rama. Lost things, faced betrayal, stayed calm, and ultimately created a happy family and respected life.

Nidhi: Yes! And there are small examples too:

- **Family first:** Padayappa protected his mother and sister, just like Rama cared for Sita and his family.
- **Forgiveness:** He forgave his uncle after saving his family, like Rama forgave Kaikeyi's mistakes.
- **Clever thinking:** He solved problems smartly, not with anger, like Rama planning the battle with Ravana.
- **Dignity and patience:** Even when insulted or disrespected, he never lost his honor, like Rama in exile.

Harshada: Haha! So if someone tries to bully me in college, I should stay calm, think smart, and act with dignity. Maybe even quote a Rajini punch line for style. 😏

Nidhi: Exactly! Like *"En Vazhi Thani Vazhi"*—find your own way, your own path, and don't let anyone steal your peace. You know, even Padayappa said it with style: *"Do not disturb me!"* 😎

Harshada: Haha! Perfect. So basically, stay calm, stay in control, and if anyone messes with you… politely show them your way.

Nidhi: Yep! That's how Padayappa walked the path of Rama. Smart, patient, dignified, and always in control.

Harshada: Hmm… so lessons from movies, coconut water, and ancient epics all together. Who knew? Life is full of guidance if you notice!

They smiled, feeling stronger and wiser. The sun was bright, the coconuts were refreshing, and the stories of Padayappa and Lord Rama made them realize: **loss, betrayal, and challenges are not the end.**

How you act, stay calm, and keep your values—that's what creates victory and prosperity.

Chapter 9

Thank You, Universe!

Nidhi and Harshada sat on the college terrace, sipping freshly made Apple Juice. The sun was warm, and the sky was clear.

Harshada: You know, after watching *Padayappa* and reading about it… I feel like we owe a huge **thank you** to so many people.

Nidhi: Haha! True. First, to the **cast and crew**. Rajinikanth, Ramya Krishnan, Soundarya… every actor gave life to the characters. K. S. Ravikumar, the director, and the writers… they created something timeless.

Harshada: Don't forget the music! A. R. Rahman… the songs made everything feel magical. And even the people behind cameras, lights, editing… they all worked so we could sit, watch, and enjoy without a worry.

Nidhi: Exactly! And then… **Maharshi Valmiki**, the sage who wrote the Ramayana, and other storytellers who shared Rama's story. Rama taught us patience, duty, dignity, and courage. Padayappa's story echoes that—so we learned life lessons while having fun.

Harshada: Yeah! In a world full of noise, viral trends, and endless media… this movie gave us **clear storytelling**, colorful drama, action, family, and values we can actually take away.

Nidhi: And we can even watch it with family, without feeling awkward. That's rare these days!

Harshada: Totally. So here's a little gratitude: **Thank you, Universe,** for Superstar Rajini Sir, the cast, the crew, the music, the writers, and even the story of Rama. You all gave us courage, inspiration, and joy in one package.

Nidhi: Yeah… for giving us lessons about life, patience, forgiveness, hard work, and staying calm… all while being entertained.

They clinked their juice glasses in a playful toast.

Harshada: To Padayappa, Lord Rama, and everyone who made both stories possible!

Nidhi: To values, style, and our own unique paths!

The two friends smiled, feeling a quiet kind of happiness.

Gratitude made them realize that even in a noisy world, stories like these were gifts—lessons wrapped in laughter, action, music, and courage.

And maybe, just maybe, they could carry a bit of Padayappa and Rama inside themselves as they faced life.

Chapter 10

WALKING OUR OWN PATH

The evening sky over **New Delhi** was painted in shades of gold and pink.

Nidhi and Harshada walked along the quiet streets, thinking about everything they had seen in the movie and read in the book.

The city around them buzzed with life, but inside, they felt calm and clear.

Nidhi: You know, after all this... I feel like we actually *can* use these lessons in real life. Not just admire Padayappa and Rama from stories.

Harshada: Totally! I was thinking the same. Like, when we start working, handling responsibilities, or making important decisions… staying calm and thinking smart is key.

Nidhi: Exactly. And friendships… we should choose friends who are supportive, honest, and positive—like Padayappa valued.

Harshada: Family too. Making time for them, showing care and patience—it really matters, just like Lord Rama did in Ayodhya.

Nidhi: Health is important too. Eat well, rest properly, and stay active… stay strong to face challenges, like Padayappa did while rebuilding his life.

Harshada: Career decisions? Work hard, stay ethical, and create our own path—*"En Vazhi Thani Vazhi"*! Not just follow what everyone else is doing.

Nidhi: Relationships also… choose wisely, respect others, forgive mistakes, and don't waste energy on revenge or anger.

Harshada: So basically, apply **values, patience, smart thinking, and self-respect** in every part of life—work, family, friends, health, and small daily choices.

Nidhi: Life won't always be easy, but if we remember **Padayappa and Lord Rama**, we can face challenges with courage, stay calm, and make choices that matter in the long run.

Harshada: Our takeaway is simple: **Work hard, stay calm, value people, be smart, and walk our own path.**

They smiled, feeling empowered. The city lights of **New Delhi** flickered on, but inside, they carried the quiet strength of the stories they loved.

Lessons from Padayappa's courage, Rama's wisdom, the movie, and the book were no longer just stories—they were **tools for living a better life**, right here, right now.

Nidhi: So readers, take what matters to you. Find your own way, face challenges with patience, and build a life full of dignity, courage, and joy.

Harshada: And enjoy the journey. Every small choice counts when you walk your own path!

A NOTE FROM THE AUTHOR

In the Spirit of Rama Rajya

This book is part of a dream — not just of writing, but of building an ***11,000-year legacy of wisdom, love, and truth.***

I dedicate it to the spirit of Rama Rajya — a time when kindness, fairness, and honesty guided life.

Like Lord Rama, may we walk the path of goodness and care.

May this story bring light, honesty, and warmth to everyone who reads it.

If you are reading this, you are now part of this long journey.

Thank you for sharing this moment with me.

"May every home be an Ayodhya.

May every heart be Rama's temple.

May truth live forever."

With love,

Ram SwaRajya

(Inspired by Rama's values of self-love, care for others, and living rightly.)

DISCLAIMER

This book is written under the pen name **Ram SwaRajya**.

The stories, ideas, and lessons come from my experiences, public knowledge, or inspiration from the **1999 Tamil movie Padayappa**.

This book is written **as a fan and common viewer**, not affiliated with the movie makers, cast, crew, or any official organization.

The purpose is to **share the wisdom and values from the movie and cultural stories**.

The content is meant to **inspire and entertain**, not to provide professional advice or verify historical facts.

For professional guidance, please consult qualified experts.

References to Indian cultural stories, including the Ramayana, are shared in a **light-hearted and imaginative way** to highlight values for today's world.

They are used with respect and are **not meant to hurt anyone's religious or cultural sentiments**.

This book was created with the help of **OpenAI's ChatGPT (free version)** and writing assistant **Grammarly (free version)**.

Spiritual Reflection: Swamiye Saranam Ayyappa

"**Swamiye Saranam Ayyappa**" is a famous chant in India.

It means **"O Lord Ayyappa, I surrender to you"** or **"I take refuge in you, Swami."**

People say it to feel courage, guidance, and calm in life.

Lord **Ayyappa** is a deity who is especially known in South India.

Millions of devotees visit the **Sabarimala temple in Kerala**, following simple rules, walking long distances, and practicing self-discipline during their pilgrimage.

These practices help focus the mind, stay patient, and build inner strength.

Saying **"Swamiye Saranam Ayyappa"** can feel like carrying a little inner strength.

It is about **trust, patience, courage, and discipline**, qualities that help us walk our own path.

Shubham